To: Jake
A magical story
for a magical you

From:

Oh no!
The wizards were in **BIG trouble!**

A wicked witch had cast an evil spell completely covering their magical kingdom in slimy and extremely smelly goo! ALL of the wizards were trapped!

4

The wizards really needed
someone to help them catch
the wicked witch,
but **who?**

The wise old grand wizard looked through his special telescope, and spotted someone who might just be able to help them.

"Quickly! Send Magical Master Owl to ask for Jake's help in saving us from the wicked witch!" shouted the wizard.

Magical Master Owl knew he had
to help so he flapped and fluttered
as swiftly as he could to find the boy
spotted through the telescope.

"WHIZZ BAM !"
Jake said, as he waved his pretend wand towards his dog Ruffles.

"Oh Ruffles you are supposed to turn into a flying dog."

Jake SO wanted to be a Wizard.

Suddenly with a flitter and a flap, Magical Master Owl squawked through Jake's window into the bedroom and explained (in his best owlish) the trouble the wizards were in, and asked a shocked Jake if he could help.

"Of course!"
said a delighted Jake.

So Magical Master Owl squawked three times, flapped his wings four times, and with a WHIZZ PUFF, a broomstick, cape and magic wand suddenly appeared!

Jake put on the cape,
picked up the wand,
and jumped on his brand
new broomstick.

Quick as a flash
they zoomed out of
Jake's window to look
for the wicked witch.

The wicked witch was flying around, covering everything and everyone with her yucky, smelly green goo.

"Wahahaha!" she cackled, "Soon the whole world will be covered in my smelly goo and there are no wizards here to stop me!"

But little did she realise that Jake was on his way.

He zoomed under bridges...

...and over houses, looking for the goo-spreading witch.

13

Suddenly Ruffles made
a big booming **bark**.
His super-smelling nose had caught
a whiff of the wicked witch, but she
was too far away for Jake
to cast a spell on her.

Jake clicked
his heels, gripped his
broomstick even tighter,
and zoomed at supersonic speed
towards the wicked witch.

Finally Jake caught up with the wicked witch.

"Who are you?" the wicked witch sneered, as she launched a massive dollop of sticky green goo at Jake.

With lightning speed
Jake waved his magic wand.
"BIZZ POP GOO I will stop you!" he shouted.
A huge brightly-coloured umbrella appeared,
deflecting all of the smelly goo.

17

The wicked witch squealed with anger, zapping another dollop of smelly green goo towards Jake.

"WHIZZ SPLAT send me your hat!" Jake shouted.

The witch's hat flew off her head, catching all of her smelly green goo. Yuck!

The witch couldn't believe what this boy wizard was doing!

"ZIP ZAP, you will be trapped in your hat!" Jake cast another spell.

The witch's goo-filled hat flew back to her, squashing down over her head, squishing her in the smelly green goo.

Hurray the wicked witch was trapped!

A triumphant Jake took the wicked witch back to the wizards' castle.

All the slippery, slimy green goo had now gone thanks to Jake breaking the bad witch's horrible spell.

The wizards were so grateful to
Jake that they let him keep the cape,
broomstick AND magic wand!

Jake finally felt like a true wizard!

The End

COLOUR
ME IN →

_____'S
BOOK OF
SPELLS